Kylie
the Carnival
Fairy

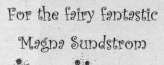

For the fairy fantastic
Magna Sundstrom

Special thanks to
Narinder Dhami

ISBN-10: 0-545-05475-3
ISBN-13: 978-0-545-05475-1

12 11 10 9 8 7 6 5 4 3 2 1   8 9 10 11 12 13/0

Printed in the U.S.A.

First Scholastic printing, June 2008

Kylie
the
Carnival
Fairy

by Daisy Meadows

SCHOLASTIC INC.

New York   Toronto   London   Auckland   Sydney
Mexico City   New Delhi   Hong Kong   Buenos Aires

Stage

Ferris Wheel

Rollercoaster
this way

Cotton Candy

GRAND

Sunny

Tunnel
of Love

COLD DRINKS

Hall of Mirrors

Spinn

Dress-Up Tent

Carnival Hat Hijinks

Fairy magic means carnival fun
While the magic hats are where they belong.
But my icy spells will cause a stir
When those hats are no longer where they were!

Band leader's hat and carnival crown
Both will go missing when I come to town.
But I'll start with the carnival master's hat
And send my goblins to capture that!

**Find the hidden letters in hats
throughout the book. Unscramble all
7 letters to spell a special carnival word!**

Contents

The Carnival Begins!

"This is so exciting!" Rachel Walker said to her best friend, Kirsty Tate. "I've never been to a real carnival before."

"And Sunnydays is the *best* carnival," Kirsty replied. "It comes to Wetherbury every summer. I'm so glad you're staying with us, so that you can visit the carnival, too."

The girls were standing with a big crowd of people, including Kirsty's parents, outside the gates of the carnival grounds. The buzz of excited chatter filled the air as everyone waited for the grand opening.

"Which ride will you go on first, girls?" asked Mr. Tate.

"I don't know," Kirsty said, peering over the gates. "There are so many!" She could see a Ferris wheel, bumper cars, spinning teacups, and lots of other rides. There were also booths of food and games like the ring toss and hook-a-duck.

"Look, Kirsty!" Rachel nudged her

friend as a man in a red coat and black top hat appeared behind the gates.

"He must be the carnival master," Kirsty explained. "It's finally time for the grand opening!"

The crowd cheered loudly.

"Ladies and gentlemen," boomed the carnival master. "Welcome to Sunnydays, the most magical carnival in the world!" He threw open the gates with a flourish. "Follow me!" Rachel and Kirsty hurried inside the carnival grounds

eagerly, the rest of the crowd close
behind them.

"Let the carnival magic begin!"
announced the carnival master, sweeping
off his top hat and pointing it at the
Ferris wheel. Immediately, the great
wheel began to turn! The crowd gasped.

Then the carnival master waved his hat at the teacups, which began to spin in a blur of bright colors.

"It *is* magic!" gasped a little girl nearby as the rides sprang to life.

Rachel and Kirsty smiled. They knew all about magic. The two girls had become friends with the fairies! They helped their tiny friends whenever wicked Jack Frost and his goblins caused trouble in Fairyland.

Just then, a loud drumbeat echoed through the air.

"It's the parade!" Kirsty cried.

There was a clash of cymbals. Then a band, led by a man in a blue uniform, marched toward the crowd. The band leader wore a tall blue hat, trimmed with gold braid. He carried a rainbow-colored baton in one hand. As the crowd cheered, he tipped his hat and twirled his baton. Right away, the band struck up a merry tune.

"This is great," Rachel said as the band marched by. "Look, there are dancers and acrobats, too!"

Dancers in blue-and-gold dresses followed the band. They held long satin ribbons in their hands, and twirled and twisted them as they danced.

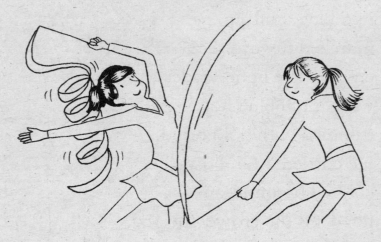

The acrobats jumped and tumbled, handing out party poppers in between cartwheels. Kirsty and Rachel

were excited when they each got
a popper.

"There are jugglers,
too!" Kirsty pointed
out suddenly.

The jugglers
wore red-and-
white jester's
hats with bells on
the ends. They each
carried colorful
juggling balls.

"Oh, no!" Rachel giggled as one of the jugglers dropped all his balls at once. "I think they need a little more practice."

Kirsty frowned as another one of the jugglers stumbled into an acrobat. "They're not very tall," she said. "Maybe they're kids. That would explain why they're not very good at juggling yet." But then Kirsty glanced down at the

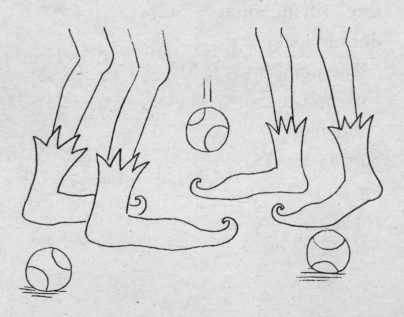

jugglers' feet. Their shoes were huge —
much too big for children's shoes!

Kirsty peered closely at the jugglers as
they paraded past. Although their hats
hid most of their faces, she realized that
they had long green noses.

"Rachel!" Kirsty whispered, her heart
pounding. "Those jugglers aren't kids.
They're goblins!"

The Goblins Make Mischief

"Oh, no!" Rachel gasped. Kirsty was right!

"Why are Jack Frost's goblins here?" Kirsty wondered aloud, counting them quickly. "Rachel, there are *eight* of them!"

"And Jack Frost has made them bigger, too," Rachel added. "They're almost as tall as we are. That must be so they don't stand out in the crowd."

"I bet they're up to no good!" Kirsty said, frowning.

"Let me present our most magical ride!" the carnival master announced just then.

"Look at the goblins," Kirsty whispered.

All eight goblins were running right toward the carnival master! As they got closer to him, the biggest goblin jumped up and knocked the top hat off his head.

The carnival master yelped in surprise, but everyone else laughed, thinking it was part of the show. One of the other goblins caught the hat as it fell. Then they all disappeared into the crowd.

"Why do the goblins want the carnival master's hat?" Kirsty asked Rachel as the shocked carnival master struggled to continue with his announcement.

"Er, as I was saying," he stammered. "This is the most important ride at the carnival!" He pointed to a huge green-and-gold sheet, which was clearly hiding something very big.

Two clowns on stilts stood on either side of the sheet, each holding a corner. There was a drumroll from the band, and then the clowns pulled away the sheet. Suddenly, the girls could see a brightly painted carousel of beautiful horses — but unlike the other rides, this one didn't start turning.

"The carousel will be working soon," the carnival master said quickly. "In the meantime, please enjoy our other wonderful rides!"

But as Kirsty and Rachel looked around the carnival, they noticed that the Ferris wheel was stopping, and that the teacups were slowing to a halt, too. What was going on?

Suddenly, out of the corner of her eye, Kirsty spotted a flash of red and white. It was

the goblins again — and this time, they were rushing toward the band leader!

"Look out!" Kirsty cried, trying to warn him.

But the band was playing too loudly for the band leader to hear. The tallest goblin jumped up and knocked the hat right off his head! Another goblin swept it up off the ground, and they all raced away.

The minute the band leader lost his hat, he also lost control of the band. The tubas and flutes sounded out of tune, the trumpeters started marching in the wrong direction, and the drummers dropped their drumsticks. The cheerful music suddenly turned into a whole lot of noise!

"Why are the goblins trying to ruin the carnival?" Rachel wondered.

"I don't know," Kirsty said with a sigh. The band had stopped playing now, and the band leader looked dazed. The carnival master rushed forward.  "Don't forget," he announced, trying to distract the crowd, "for the closing day parade, we want you all to dress up. The boy or girl with the best costume will be crowned carnival king or queen with our carnival crown!"

Just then, Rachel and Kirsty heard the *clip-clop* of hooves behind them. Everyone turned to see two women in sparkly pink costumes riding white ponies. The

women carried a blue velvet cushion
between them, and on top of the
cushion sat the carnival crown, covered
with jewels and feathers.

"I now declare Sunnydays Carnival

officially open!" the carnival master cried
proudly.

The crowd cheered and scattered to
explore the carnival.

"We have to find out what the goblins
are up to," Rachel said anxiously.

Kirsty nodded, shivering. "It suddenly feels cold, doesn't it?" she asked, her teeth chattering.

Rachel nodded and rubbed her arms. "It's been warm all day until now," she said, frowning.

At that moment, Kirsty noticed a clown in a baggy yellow costume and

curly green wig standing nearby. He was staring at the carnival crown.

Kirsty nudged Rachel. "Look," she whispered, pointing. "There's something familiar about that clown."

Rachel peered at the clown. Then, with a start, she noticed frosty icicles hanging from his chin. "Kirsty," Rachel gasped. "That's Jack Frost!"

Kylie Pops In

Kirsty stared at Jack Frost in horror. "He used his magic to make himself as big as the goblins," she whispered to Rachel.

At that moment, the goblins reappeared. Trying to juggle, they quickly surrounded the carnival crown.

In the meantime, Jack Frost had
created an icy wind, which swept him up
and carried him through the air. But
only Kirsty and Rachel noticed as he
zoomed toward the crown. Everybody
else was too busy watching the goblin
jugglers!

The girls saw
Jack Frost
snatch the
crown from its
cushion and
disappear
from sight. The
goblins gathered
up their juggling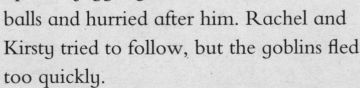
balls and hurried after him. Rachel and
Kirsty tried to follow, but the goblins fled
too quickly.

"The crown!" gasped one of the women on the ponies. "Where did it go?"

"Maybe it fell off the cushion," the other woman suggested, looking around.

"Now Jack Frost has the carnival master's hat, the band leader's hat, and the carnival crown!" Kirsty cried, biting her lip. "What's he going to do with them?"

"Let's find out," Rachel suggested.

Kirsty turned to her parents, who were chatting with some friends. "Mom, can Rachel and I go on the rides?"

Mrs. Tate nodded. "We'll meet you at the front gate in half an hour," she replied.

The girls grinned and hurried after the goblins.

Suddenly, Rachel felt a tingling in her fingers. She glanced down and realized that she was still holding her party popper. And now it seemed to be shaking . . . all by itself!

Suddenly, the party popper exploded in a shower of glitter. Rachel jumped as streamers shot into the air. "Oh!" she cried in surprise.

A fairy hovered in the glitter, beaming at the girls. As the streamers floated to the ground, the fairy flew to Kirsty's shoulder. Her skirt, striped in all the colors of the rainbow, billowed around her as she landed.

"Hello, girls!" the fairy called, pushing a few strands of dark brown hair out of her eyes. "I'm Kylie the Carnival Fairy!"

"Hello," Rachel gasped, still startled.

"As Carnival Fairy, it's my job to make sure the Sunnydays Carnival is a huge success," Kylie explained. "But Jack Frost is trying to ruin everything!"

"Why?" asked Kirsty.

"Because he got bored in his ice castle," Kylie said, sighing. "So he decided to spoil everybody's fun."

"What about the hats?" Rachel chimed in.

Kylie winked at the girls. "The hats are magical!" she said with a grin.  "The carnival master's hat makes all the rides run smoothly."

"No wonder

the carousel wasn't working,"
Kirsty said.

Kylie nodded. "The band leader's
magical hat makes the carnival music
perfect," she went on. "That's why the
band can't play in tune anymore. And
the carnival crown makes sure that the
Sunnydays Carnival ends happily and
can move on to the next town."

"So if we
can't get back
the hats, the
carnival will be
ruined for
everyone!"
Rachel cried.

"We can't let
that happen,"
Kirsty added.

"I knew you'd help me, girls," Kylie declared happily. "Now, where are Jack Frost and his goblins?"

"They went that way," Rachel said.

.As the girls looked into the distance,
Kirsty spotted a flash of red and white.

"There's a goblin," she said excitedly,
pointing him out to Rachel and Kylie.
"And he has the carnival master's hat!"

A Spooky Ride

"After him!" Kylie cried, sliding into Rachel's pocket and out of sight.

The girls hurried toward the goblin. But before they could get too close, he spotted them.

"It's those pesky girls!" he shouted to his two goblin friends. "Quick, hide!"

The three goblins immediately ran off, followed closely by the girls.

As the goblins passed the haunted house, one of them skidded to a halt. "In here!" he shouted. Ignoring the sign that said BROKEN — PLEASE COME BACK LATER, the three goblins rushed inside.

Kirsty and Rachel both blinked as they saw a shimmer of magic. Suddenly, all the lights outside the haunted house came on.

"The carnival master's magical hat is making the ride work," Kylie explained.

The giggling goblins climbed into the front car of the train inside the haunted house. Rachel and Kirsty just managed to jump into the car behind them as the train pulled away.

When the train turned the corner, the girls saw spider webs and bats hanging from dark trees. A cold wind howled

around them. Rachel and Kirsty knew it
was only a sound effect, but the goblins
had stopped giggling and were muttering
to one another, scared.

"Whoooooooo!" a ghost jumped out from
behind a tree, moaning loudly. The goblins
shrieked with fright.

"I don't think the goblins are enjoying
the ride!" Kirsty laughed.

As the train rattled around another corner, a loud, creaking sound filled the air.

"What's that?" the goblins wailed. Then they screamed as a nearby coffin swung open, and a vampire with long, sharp fangs leaned out.

Eventually, the train shot back out through the doors and came to a stop. Still trembling with fear, the goblins leaped out of the train and ran away.

"They're heading for the log flume," Kylie said. "Follow them, quick!"

The log flume wasn't working. It had a
NO ENTRY sign outside. But once again,
the goblins ignored the sign and jumped
into one of the floating, log-shaped
boats. Immediately, there was a dazzling
flash of magic.

"The carnival master's hat is at work again," Rachel said.

Sure enough, water began to tumble and splash along the waterways, and the goblins' little boat floated away.

Kirsty turned to Rachel and Kylie. "What are we going to do?" she asked.

Rachel was staring at the water. "I have an idea!" she announced.

The Goblins Outwitted!

"What is it?" Kylie asked eagerly.

"Look!" Rachel pointed at the ride. At the bottom of one of the waterways was a long slide.

"The goblins will be coming down that slide soon," Rachel explained. "If we stand at the bottom, we can try to grab the hat as they go by."

"Perfect!" Kylie exclaimed.

The goblins were out of sight for now, but the girls and Kylie could hear them squealing with delight. Quickly, they hurried over to the bottom of the slide and waited.

"They're at the top of the slide," Rachel whispered as the goblins' boat floated into sight. "Get ready!"

At that moment, the log-shaped boat tipped over the

edge and shot down the slide toward the girls. "Yee-hah!" the goblins yelled, waving their arms in the air. They were sitting one behind the other in the little boat. Rachel, Kirsty, and Kylie could see that the goblin with the carnival master's hat was in the back. The boat zoomed down to the bottom of the slide. Kirsty was closest to the water, and as the boat splashed past, she reached out and snatched the hat right out of the goblin's hand!

"Give that back!" the goblin yelled
furiously. "Stop the boat!" But there was
nothing they could do. The boat swept
on along the waterways, taking the
angry goblins with it.

"Good job!" Kylie laughed as Kirsty
shook drops of water off the hat.
"Now, let's take that hat back
where it belongs."

Kylie slipped into
Rachel's pocket
again. They all
hurried off to
the main tent
in the middle of the
carnival grounds.
The carnival master stood in the tent's
entrance with the band leader, looking
very unhappy.

"I think we might have to close the
carnival," the carnival master was
saying. "Too many rides aren't
working!"

"We're just in time," Kirsty whispered.

"But how are we going to give back
the hat?" Rachel asked. "They'll want to
know where we found it!"

"Kylie, could you make us fairy-size?"

Kirsty asked quietly. "And the hat, too?
Then we'll be able to return it without
being seen."

Kylie nodded. Quickly, the girls slipped
behind the tent, where Kylie waved her
wand over them. Rachel, Kirsty, and the
hat all shrank to fairy-size. Then,
carrying the tiny hat, the girls and Kylie
flew back to the tent entrance.

They waited until the carnival master
went to check on the
rides. Then they
flew inside and
put the hat on
his desk.
Kylie waved
her wand — and
the hat grew back
to its usual size!
Then they fluttered
back outside, and Kylie's magic soon
turned Rachel and Kirsty into normal
girls again.

A moment later, they heard the
carnival master returning to the tent.

"We'll have to close down," he said to
the band leader. "I'll make an
announcement."

Kirsty, Rachel, and Kylie peeked
around the side of the tent as the carnival
master went inside. "My
hat!" he exclaimed.
"How did that get
here?" He picked up
the hat and put
it on.
Rachel and Kirsty
beamed at each
other as suddenly,
all around them,
they heard the whirr
of rides starting up again. The Ferris
wheel was moving, the teacups started
spinning, and the bumper cars were
crashing into one another.

"Look, even the carousel's turning!"
Rachel pointed out.

"Everything's working again!" the band leader exclaimed in amazement from outside the tent.

"That's wonderful!" the carnival master gasped, rushing outside to see. "It's almost like magic!"

Kylie laughed as she turned to Rachel and Kirsty. "It *is* magic!" she said. "And I couldn't have gotten the magic hat back without the two of you." She smiled at the girls. "Now I must head back to Fairyland to tell everyone the good news."

"We'd better go and find my mom and dad," Kirsty said.

Rachel nodded. "But we'll be back tomorrow to help you find the other hats," she promised Kylie.

"Thank you, girls!" Kylie called, waving as she disappeared in a dazzling shower of sparkles.

"Jack Frost is so mean," said Kirsty as she and Rachel headed for the front gate. "He hates to see people having fun."

"Well, we can't let him ruin the carnival!" Rachel said, determined. "I wonder if we'll find another hat tomorrow?"

A Musical Mess

Contents

Mirror Magic

"I'm so glad Mom and Dad let us come to the Sunnydays Carnival early today," Kirsty remarked as she and Rachel walked around the carnival grounds. It was the second day of the carnival, and the sun shined brightly in the clear blue sky. "It gives us more time to look for the magical hats."

"Well, you did tell them we wanted to go on all the rides!" Rachel said with a grin.

"Yes, but Dad says we have to meet up later so we can all go on the roller coaster together." Kirsty laughed. "That's his favorite!"

Suddenly, a loud clatter made Rachel clap her hands over her ears. "What's that noise?" she cried. "It's terrible!"

"It's the band," Kirsty said sadly. "No wonder it sounds awful — they don't have the band leader's magical hat!"

"Look!" Rachel pointed at the stage. "The dancers are putting on a show. That's why the band is playing."

The girls walked toward the stage, but as they got closer, they saw that everything was going wrong. Not only was the band playing out of tune, but it was out of time, too. The dancers couldn't keep up with the rhythm, so they kept bumping into one another.

"The band leader looks upset," whispered Kirsty.

Rachel saw that the band leader was conducting the music and wincing at every wrong note. Only a few people were watching the show, and some of them had their fingers in their ears!

Just then, the carnival master hurried onto the stage, looking flustered. "Thank you, dancers," he said loudly, "The show's over, ladies and gentlemen!" He began to clap.

A few members of the audience clapped halfheartedly, as they began to move away.

The carnival master shook his head in despair. "I don't know what's going on today," he said, staring at the dancers. "You're usually so good!" He sighed. "Come on, I think you need a break. I'll take you to the refreshment tent for a snack."

Looking glum, the dancers followed him off the stage.

"I think you'd better go, too," the band leader said, looking sadly at his musicians. "We'll try again later."

"The music won't sound right until we get the band leader's hat back," Kirsty said. She and Rachel watched the gloomy musicians put down their instruments and leave.

"We should start looking for the hat right away," Rachel suggested. "I bet the goblins are still around here somewhere, enjoying the carnival."

"Oh, but remember what the fairies always say." Kirsty grinned at her friend. "We should let the magic come to us!"

Rachel laughed. "In that case, why don't we have some carnival fun ourselves?" she said.

"Good idea!" Kirsty agreed.

The girls wandered around the carnival grounds, enjoying the sunshine. They passed a dress-up tent, and a cotton candy booth. Then they spotted the hall of mirrors.

"Oh, I love this!" Rachel said eagerly. "Let's go in."

Kirsty swung open the door, and the girls stepped inside. It was dark for a split-second, but as the door closed, the lights came on. The girls were surrounded by hundreds of Kirstys and Rachels, reflected in the tall mirrors all around them!

"This is weird!" Rachel laughed, turning from side to side. Her reflections turned, too. "Look, Kirsty!" She raised her arms, and hundreds of Rachels raised their arms, too. Before Kirsty could speak, there was a sudden pop, and a burst of colorful glitter surrounded the girls as it floated to the ground. "Where did that come from?" Kirsty gasped in surprise. The glitter was reflected in all the mirrors, and the girls felt as if they were surrounded by dazzling fireworks.

"Look," Rachel cried. "Fairies!"

There, dancing in the mirrors, the girls could see hundreds of tiny fairies. Their wings fluttered and shimmered with light. It was such a magical sight that

Kirsty and Rachel could hardly believe their eyes!

Then Rachel laughed. "Oh, look, it's not hundreds of fairies," she told Kirsty. "It's just Kylie!"

Suspicious Scouts

"Hello, girls!" called a tiny voice behind them. The girls turned to see Kylie smiling happily. "I'm so glad to see you," she went on. "I can tell that the band leader's hat isn't far away!"

"Great!" Kirsty said eagerly. "Let's keep our eyes open."

"First we have to find our way out of here," said Rachel, looking around in confusion at all the mirrors.

"The exit door must have a mirror on the back, to hide it," Kirsty said with a frown.

"I'll help," Kylie said, smiling and waving her wand. A shower of magic pink sparkles flew from the wand. They surrounded one of the mirrors in a glittering frame of fairy dust.

Rachel hurried over and pushed the mirror. It swung open, and as the girls made their way outside, Kylie flew down to Kirsty's shoulder and hid behind her hair.

Kirsty and Rachel stood outside the hall of mirrors, looking around for a sign of anything unusual. Rachel turned and glanced at the dress-up tent. A group of Cub Scouts wearing dark blue uniforms were gathered just inside. They squealed with delight as they tried on different outfits and had their faces painted.

Rachel was about to turn away, when she realized that something wasn't quite right. For one thing, there were no carnival workers in the tent — the Cub Scouts were painting one another's faces! Rachel looked a little more closely.

"Look at those Cub Scouts," she said to Kirsty and Kylie.

At that moment, one of the Cub Scouts, who was dressed up like a witch, rushed forward and pushed another Cub Scout out of the face-painting chair. This one was still wearing his Cub Scout uniform, but he had an orange-and-black striped tiger's face.

"It's my turn now!" yelled the first Cub Scout, sitting down and whipping off his witch's hat. Now Kylie, Rachel, and Kirsty could all see that his face was green!

"He's a goblin!" Rachel breathed.

"They're *all* goblins!" Kirsty added.

The girls carefully edged closer to the tent. They could see that the goblins had been very busy. One was dressed in a monkey suit, with a monkey mask. Another was wearing a black suit with white bones on it — he looked like a skeleton! Rachel noticed that his face had been painted in black and white to look like a skull.

"Look at the one doing the face painting!" Kirsty whispered to Rachel and Kylie. They couldn't help laughing when they realized that the goblin looked exactly like Jack Frost! He wore a cloak over his shoulders and had a spiky wig and beard. He had painted them white, to look like Jack Frost's icy hair.

Now he was glaring at the witch goblin who had sat down to have his face painted. "You don't need painting!" he snapped. "Everybody knows witches are supposed to be green."

Suddenly, through the open doorway of the tent, Rachel spotted the band leader's blue-and-gold hat on the table. "There's the hat!" she whispered excitedly, pointing it out.

"Girls, if I make you fairy-size, maybe we can slip in and get the hat without being spotted," Kylie whispered.

Rachel and Kirsty nodded. Kylie waved her wand, and soon the girls were tiny fairies with glittering wings on their backs. Then all three friends flew cautiously toward the dress-up tent.

Frightening Faces

Just before the friends reached the
entrance of the tent, the tiger-faced
goblin hurried over to the table. To the
girls' dismay, he grabbed the band
leader's hat and jammed it firmly
on his head. The he marched out of
the tent.

"After him!" whispered Kirsty.

The tiger-faced goblin started to hurry off across the grounds.

"Where are you going?" the skeleton goblin shouted after him.

The first goblin stuck his tongue out. "I'm going to have some fun on the rides!" he yelled.

He looks awfully silly in his Cub Scout uniform, with his tiger's face, the band leader's hat on his head, and his tongue sticking out, Kirsty thought. Rachel, Kylie, and Kirsty couldn't help laughing.

"I want to have fun, too!" roared the skeleton goblin. He dropped the pirate costume he'd been about to try on.

"So do we!" shouted the other goblins, throwing down the paint tubes and costumes they were holding.

"Let's go!" Rachel whispered. The three friends flew after the goblins, wondering which ride they would head for.

But the tiger-faced goblin stopped
when he saw the HALL OF MIRRORS sign.
"What's a hall of mirrors?" he asked.

"Oh, you're silly!" scoffed the goblin in
the monkey suit. "Everyone knows what
a hall of mirrors is!"

"Well, what is it?" asked the first goblin.

"It's . . . er . . ." the monkey-faced goblin's voice trailed away. He looked very uncomfortable.

"He doesn't know!" scoffed the witch goblin. "Let's go inside and find out." He pulled open the door, and the goblins began fighting to get in first.

"We'll slip inside before they close the door," Kylie whispered to the girls. "One, two three, go!"

As the door swung shut, Kylie, Rachel, and Kirsty swooped forward and managed to dart inside.

As before, the lights came on once the door closed. Hovering high overhead, Rachel, Kirsty, and Kylie could see the goblins' painted faces reflected hundreds of times in the mirrors. The goblins could see them, too — and they stared at the mirrors in alarm!

"Help!" shrieked the tiger-faced goblin. "Where have all these scary monsters come from?"

"Get me out of here!" roared the Jack Frost goblin. "I can see hundreds of tigers!"

"Uh-oh, Jack Frost's here, too — dozens of him!" the monkey-faced goblin yelled in terror. "And he looks really angry!"

Tricked Again!

Kirsty turned to Kylie and Rachel.
"The goblins don't realize that they're
looking at their own reflections." She
laughed. "They're scaring themselves
silly!"

"I can see skeletons!" moaned the
witch goblin. "Hundreds of horrible
skeletons that have come to life!"

He backed away from the mirrors and slammed right into the tiger-faced goblin. They bumped into each other so hard that the band leader's hat fell to the ground.

Suddenly, the tiger-faced goblin shouted, "Hey! Those monsters aren't monsters!" He gasped. "They're *us*!" And he pointed at the mirror closest to him.

"The tiger's pointing at us!" gasped the monkey-suited goblin in terror.

"That's because it's ME!" the tiger-faced goblin shouted impatiently. "It's my reflection!"

Kirsty was laughing so hard she thought she would burst, and Kylie was giggling, too.

But Rachel was staring at the hat on the floor. "Now's our chance," she whispered. "Together we can lift it!"

Kylie and Kirsty stopped laughing and nodded. In the meantime, the goblins stared more closely at the mirrors and finally realized that the tiger-faced goblin was right.

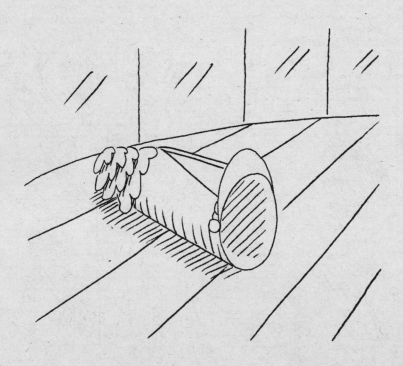

"I knew it all along!" said the Jack Frost goblin. "What a bunch of silly fools you are!"

"Who are you calling a fool?" snapped the tiger-faced goblin.

Rachel, Kirsty, and Kylie fluttered down over the goblins' heads toward the hat. Just as they were almost within reach, the tiger-faced goblin snatched it up! Kylie and the girls had to zoom behind a mirror to hide.

"I've found the door!" yelled the witch goblin suddenly, pushing it open. The goblins tumbled out into the sunshine, still arguing loudly. The door slammed shut behind them. This time, Kylie and the girls weren't quick enough to fly out.

"We almost had the hat that time!" Rachel said, sighing.

"We can't give up," Kirsty said firmly. "Kylie, can you make us human-size again, so we can open the door?"

Kylie nodded. In a shower of magic sparkles from her wand, the girls shot up to their normal size. Then they raced out of the hall of mirrors with Kylie perched on Rachel's shoulder.

"There go the goblins!" Rachel said, pointing ahead.

"It looks like they're heading for the teacups," added Kirsty.

The girls hurried after them. The carnival was even busier now than it had been earlier. All the rides the girls passed were full, including the carousel. Rachel smiled to see children sitting on the pretty wooden horses, beaming happily as they whizzed around and around. But then she frowned. "The carousel music sounds awfully squeaky and out of tune!" she remarked.

"So does the music on the bumper cars," Kirsty agreed as they hurried along.

"Music is very important in making sure that everyone enjoys the carnival," Kylie sighed. "That's why we have to get the band leader's hat back right away!"

Giddy Goblins

The goblins looked excited as they headed for a large pink teacup. They all climbed in and waited for the ride to start.

"What now?" asked Rachel, staring at the tiger-faced goblin wearing the magical hat.

Kirsty had been thinking hard. "I have an idea," she said slowly, as the ride started up. "Kylie, could you make the teacup spin even faster than usual?"

Kylie's eyes twinkled. "Oh, yes," she replied. The goblins were enjoying themselves as the ride turned and their teacup began to spin. Smiling, Kylie pointed her wand at the goblins' cup and sent sparkling fairy dust rushing toward it. The teacup began to spin faster.

"Hooray!" shouted the goblins. "This is fun!"

"That's not fast enough!" Kylie laughed and waved her wand again.

Now the teacup began to whiz around even more quickly. Rachel and Kirsty could see that the goblins were starting to look even greener than usual! The teacup was moving so fast that the tiger-faced goblin was forced to hang on to the side. Kylie raised her wand one last time, and a shower of sparkles made the teacup spin super-fast. The goblins were almost a blur! The witch's hat was snug on a goblin's head, but the band leader's hat wasn't. The tiger-faced goblin put up a hand to grab the band leader's hat, but he was too late.

The hat flew off his head and
went spinning through the air.
"My hat!" the tiger-faced
goblin shrieked.
"Stop the teacup!"
moaned the witch goblin.
"I want to get off!"
Rachel hurried over and picked up the
hat as Kylie lifted her wand to slow down
the teacup again.
Then the girls
watched as the ride
stopped and the
goblins climbed off.
They were so dizzy
that they couldn't
walk straight. Rachel
giggled as they bumped into each other.
"Thank goodness we got the hat," said

Kylie. "But now we need to take it to the band leader. It's almost time for the afternoon parade."

The girls hurried off to the tent next to the stage. The band leader was standing outside with the carnival master. As the girls and Kylie approached, they could hear them talking.

"It's time for the show," the carnival master was saying. "Look, there are lots of people in the audience, and the dancers and the band have had a break now. I'm sure they'll be much better this time."

The band leader nodded, but he looked doubtful as he went into the tent where his musicians were tuning their instruments. Rachel, Kirsty, and Kylie followed him. They peeked through the tent flap and saw the band lining up, with the dancers behind them.

"How are we going to give back the hat?" Rachel whispered.

"The band leader hasn't picked up his baton yet," Kirsty said, noticing it on the table. "Kylie, maybe you could make the hat appear right next to it?"

Kylie winked. With a flick of her wand, she made the hat shrink. Then she sent the tiny hat whizzing through the tent flap and over to the table. It landed neatly next to the baton. With a final wave of her wand, Kylie made the hat grow back to its normal size.

"Perfect!" Kirsty said, beaming.

The band leader hurried over to the table to pick up his baton, and stopped in surprise when he saw his hat lying next to it. "My hat!" he gasped. "How did that get there?" Smiling from ear to ear, the band leader put on his hat, picked up his baton, and cleared his throat. "Now, let's try and play a bit better than we did earlier," he said to the band.

Looking nervous, the band leader took his place at the head of the parade. He raised his baton. The trumpeters played a fanfare as they all marched toward the tent opening. Rachel, Kirsty, and Kylie stepped back to watch the parade.

The band broke into a lively tune, played in perfect time, and the girls grinned at each other. Onstage, the dancers twirled their ribbons and performed their steps expertly, without missing a beat. The audience began to applaud loudly.

"Everything is back to normal!" Rachel said with a sigh of relief. She turned to glance at the carousel. The horses were still spinning, and the music sounded sweet and tuneful now.

"Not quite everything!" Kylie replied. "The goblins still have the carnival crown. And without that, the carnival won't be able to move on to the next town. Lots of other boys and girls will miss out on carnival fun!"

"Don't worry, Kylie," Kirsty said. "We'll do our best to find the crown."

Kylie smiled gratefully. "Thank you,"

she said. "But it's your carnival, too! So go and enjoy yourselves now. I'll return to Fairyland and tell the king and queen the latest news. They'll be so happy to hear that we only have one magic hat left to find!" She waved. "See you tomorrow."

Rachel and Kirsty waved back as Kylie disappeared in a shower of sparkles.

"It's time to meet Mom and Dad at the roller coaster," said Kirsty.

"Well, Kylie *did* tell us to go and enjoy ourselves," Rachel replied with a grin. "And tomorrow, we'll be on the lookout for the carnival crown!"

The Carnival Crown

Contents

Cats and Clowns

"I can't believe it's the last day of the carnival!" Kirsty said, slipping on her mask and turning to her friend. "How do I look, Rachel?"

"Awesome!" Rachel laughed.

Both girls were wearing costumes, getting ready for the carnival's closing-day parade.

The parade and fireworks were taking place that evening. The girls had visited the carnival earlier in the day, hoping to find the missing carnival crown. Unfortunately, they hadn't seen a single goblin or any sign of the stolen crown!

Now Rachel and Kirsty were back in Kirsty's room, both dressed as black cats in black pants, black shirts, and black velvet masks. Mrs. Tate had made them each a fluffy tail, and the girls had drawn whiskers on their faces with black eyeliner.

"Pearl doesn't look very impressed!" Kirsty laughed and glanced at her cat, who was snoozing on her bed.

Rachel smiled, then frowned nervously. "I'm excited about the parade, but I'm worried," she said. "If we don't find the crown, the Sunnydays Carnival won't be able to move on to the next town."

Kirsty nodded. "Let's hope we have some luck tonight," she said.

"Are you ready, girls?" Mr. Tate called.

"Coming!" Kirsty yelled. She and Rachel hurried downstairs.

Kirsty's parents were dressed up as clowns in baggy suits and red noses. They both clapped and cheered when they saw the girls in their costumes.

"You two look great," said Mrs. Tate.

"So do you!" Kirsty said, giggling.

"Just don't trip over your tails," Mr. Tate added as they headed out the door.

The carnival was in full swing when they arrived. Dusk was falling, and all the booths were brightly lit. The weather had turned cold when the sun went down, but there were still long lines of people waiting to go on every ride. Rachel and Kirsty were glad that their costumes were cozy!

"It's not going to be easy to spot the goblins in this crowd!" Rachel whispered.

"We'll just have to keep our eyes open," Kirsty replied, glancing around. "Oh, look, Rachel — hook-a-duck!" She pointed at the booth where little, plastic yellow ducks were bobbing in a tub of water. "Let's try it!"

"We're going to get some coffee," said Mrs. Tate. "We'll meet you at the fireworks display later, OK, girls?" Kirsty and Rachel nodded. They hurried over to the hook-a-duck booth as Mr. and Mrs. Tate walked off across the carnival grounds.

Kirsty paid the man behind the booth, and he handed each of the girls a fishing rod. There was a hook on the end of the line, so that she and Rachel could try and catch the ducks.

Rachel concentrated on the duck floating closest to her. It bobbed away a few times, but she finally managed to catch it. As she pulled it toward her, she heard a tiny voice cry, "Hello, Rachel!"

Rachel was so surprised that she almost dropped the duck! Then she looked more closely and saw Kylie perched on the little duck's back.

Rachel grinned and nudged Kirsty. "I've hooked something better than a duck." She laughed. "Look!"

Quickly, the girls put down their fishing rods and the duck. They moved away from the stall to talk to Kylie.

"Jack Frost is here!" Kylie said breathlessly, fluttering onto Rachel's shoulder. "He thinks his goblins haven't been causing enough trouble at the carnival, so he came to keep an eye on them. And . . . he has the carnival crown!"

"That's why it's so cold tonight!" exclaimed Kirsty. Kylie nodded.

"Have you seen any goblins, Kylie?" Rachel asked. But as soon as she asked, she saw three small figures in jester hats hurrying toward the tunnel of love.

"Look!" Rachel gasped, as she spotted their green faces. "Goblins!"

Finding Jack Frost

"Nice job, Rachel!" cheered Kylie.

"Let's follow them," Kirsty suggested.

The three goblins jumped into the front car of the train outside the tunnel of love. Rachel, Kirsty, and Kylie quickly climbed into another car a little further back. The goblins didn't even notice!

The train slowly set off into the tunnel.
It was dark inside, so the girls took off
their masks and stuffed them in their
pockets.

As the train chugged on, they saw that
the tunnel of love was based around the
four seasons. First, they traveled through
the spring area, where there were pretty
gardens full of daffodils and bluebells.

Summer came next, and the scenes showed a park with people picnicking and sunbathing. A park bench stood under a pretty arch of roses. The air felt warmer! In the autumn section, it became cooler again. The girls could see fake trees with red, orange, and gold leaves.

The winter scene came last. It was the coldest of all! Here, there was fake snow on the ground and people ice skating and sledding. The girls could see models of snowmen and frosty trees scattered around, too.

The train slowed down as it reached a curve in the track. The girls were surprised to see the goblins leap off and disappear behind one of the painted scenes!

"Quick!" whispered Rachel. "We'd better follow them."

The girls stepped down from their train car and hurried to hide behind a plastic tree.

"Hurry up, you fools!" a voice bellowed from the shadows. Kylie and the girls jumped. They peeked out from behind the tree to see Jack Frost sitting on a throne of ice nearby!

"He's wearing the carnival crown!"

whispered Kirsty in excitement. Jack Frost glared at his goblins. "You're having too much fun!" he snapped. "You should be ruining the carnival for the humans, not enjoying it yourselves!"

"Maybe we can creep behind the scenery, sneak up to the throne, and grab the crown right off his head!" Rachel suggested quietly.

"Good idea," Kylie agreed. Rachel and Kirsty began to edge carefully toward the throne.

"WELL?" Jack Frost roared.

"I have an idea for how to ruin the carnival," one goblin volunteered. "We could steal all the candy apples and eat them!"

"We can frighten the little children!" another shouted.

"And we could put wet paint on all the horses on the carousel!" suggested another goblin eagerly.

"Excellent!" Jack Frost declared, rubbing his hands together gleefully. "I'll keep the carnival crown here, so that those pesky fairies can't get their hands on it!"

The goblins cheered. Then, snickering, they all ran back outside to the carnival. Rachel and Kirsty had just reached the throne, and they could see the crown poking above the back of it.

"Can you reach it, Rachel?" Kylie whispered.

"I'll try," Rachel replied, cautiously stretching out her hand. But suddenly, the crown was whisked away! Jack Frost leaped to his feet. The girls jumped, and Kylie almost tumbled off Rachel's shoulder.

"Thought you could fool me, didn't you?" Jack Frost sneered, peering around the throne at them. "Well, you can't! I knew you were there the whole time!"

"We want the crown!" Rachel cried.

"Yes, you have to give it back!" Kirsty added bravely.

But Jack Frost only laughed. Then he pointed his wand at the girls and fired two ice bolts!

Ice Lightning

Rachel and Kirsty managed to dart out of the way just in time. When they looked again, Jack Frost had jumped into the last car of another train. As it disappeared around the corner, he gave the girls and Kylie a cheerful wave.

"After him!" cried Kirsty. The girls rushed out of the tunnel of love.

As soon as they were back outside, they realized that the goblins had already started their plan to ruin everything.

"A jester stole my candy apple!" sobbed one little boy. A little girl complained that her dress was covered in paint. Kylie and the girls wondered what to do next. Just then, they saw a goblin jester pop out from behind a tree and shout BOO! at a little girl. She burst into tears.

"The goblins are being horrible!" Kirsty said, frowning.

Rachel nodded. "We need to get back the carnival crown — and fast," she said firmly.

"It won't be easy," Kylie pointed out. "Everyone's in costume, so Jack Frost will be hard to spot."

Suddenly, there was a loud *BANG!* "Oh!" Rachel yelped in surprise. She glanced up and saw a trail of silver sparks across the sky. "It's not time for the fireworks yet," she murmured.

"Those aren't fireworks," Kylie cried. "It's one of Jack Frost's bolts of ice lightning!"

"It came from over there," Kirsty said, pointing toward the log flume.

Quickly, the girls dashed over to the
ride. Sure enough, Jack
Frost was there.
He was using his
magic to freeze all
the water in the log
flume waterways.

"Oh, no,"
Kirsty said, with
a sigh. "He found a
new way to ruin
the carnival!"

Looking very pleased with
himself, Jack Frost marched away.
Rachel, Kylie, and Kirsty followed him,
careful not to be spotted.

"I bet he's looking for another ride to
freeze!" said Rachel.

Jack Frost joined the line for the Ferris wheel. He stared up at it, his eyes shining. "He can't freeze that, can he?" Kirsty asked.

"I don't know," Kylie replied, sounding worried. "Let's get in line behind him. Girls, you should put your masks back on, so Jack Frost won't recognize you."

Rachel and Kirsty slipped their masks on and stepped into line. "Just one quick ride," Jack Frost was muttering. "I've always wanted to go on a Ferris wheel. The goblins will never know!" He looked around guiltily, to make sure no goblins were watching. Kirsty and Rachel's hearts pounded as he glanced past them, but he didn't recognize them behind their masks.

"He's going on the Ferris wheel!" Rachel whispered.

"We'll go, too!" Kirsty replied.

Looking excited, Jack Frost climbed into a car when he reached the front of the line. The girls and Kylie jumped into the next one, and the Ferris wheel began to turn.

Rachel glanced upward. Jack Frost's car was above theirs as they were lifted into the air. But Rachel realized that once they got past the top of the Ferris wheel and started to move back down, Jack Frost would be below them. *If we had something to hook the crown with,* Rachel thought, *we could lift it right off Jack Frost's head!*

Suddenly, Rachel spotted the hook-a-duck booth nearby. "I have an idea!" she

exclaimed. "Kylie, could you use your magic to make a fishing rod with a big hook at the end of the line — like the ones for hook-a-duck?"

"Oh!" Kirsty looked excited. "You mean, we can hook a crown!"

"No problem," Kylie said, laughing. She fluttered into the air and waved her wand. With a flash of sparkles, a shiny gold fishing rod appeared in Rachel's hands.

"We're going over the top of the wheel," Kirsty announced. "Now we're above Jack Frost."

Rachel took off her mask and leaned forward, trying to catch the carnival crown with the hook on the end of her fishing line. She came close, but the

wind kept blowing the hook the wrong way. Then, with a grin, Kylie fluttered down, gently caught the hook, and attached it to the crown.

Holding her breath, Rachel began to lift the crown off Jack Frost's head.

A Queen Is Crowned

Jack Frost didn't notice a thing as Rachel pulled the crown upward. He was having too much fun on the ride!

"That was great, Rachel," Kirsty whispered, grabbing the crown off the hook.

Kylie beamed at the girls.

"Now we can make sure the carnival ends happily," she said. "We'll be just in time for the crowning ceremony!"

All the rides were coming to a stop now. The parade had started. Soon it would be time for the carnival king or queen to be crowned! Once the Ferris wheel stopped, the girls jumped out of their car. Rachel glanced nervously at Jack Frost, but he still hadn't noticed that the crown was missing.

Just then, a goblin hurried up to him. "The crown!" he shouted, pointing at Jack Frost's head. "Where is it?"

Jack Frost clapped his hands to his head and realized that the crown wasn't there. Furiously, he spun around. His icy glare met Rachel's. Her heart sinking, Rachel remembered that she hadn't put her mask back on.

"You again!" Jack Frost shouted. He spotted the crown in Kirsty's hands. "I want that crown!"

"Run!" cried Kylie.

The girls took off. They headed for the main stage, where the crowning ceremony was supposed to take place. Jack Frost raced after them.

"The carnival master's onstage," Rachel panted. "We're almost there!"

At the same time, the girls could hear Jack Frost chanting a spell behind them. "You girls can't escape from me. These balls will stop you, wait and see!" he cried.

As the girls passed the bottle toss booth, a bucket of balls overturned. The balls rolled and bounced across the grass, right under the girls' feet. Rachel slipped, and Kirsty stumbled. The crown flew out of

Kirsty's hands and sailed through the air toward the stage.

"Oh, no!" Rachel cried as Jack Frost raced after it.

Jack Frost caught the crown at the edge of the stage, just as the carnival master stepped up to make an announcement.

"I'm sorry to say that the carnival crown is missing," he said sadly. "But the carnival king or queen will still receive free tickets to next year's carnival."

As the carnival master spoke, a spotlight came on. It lit up Jack Frost in a

blaze of white light. He stood, blinking,
with the crown in his hand.

"The carnival crown!" The carnival
master gasped, hurrying over to Jack
Frost. "You found it! That's wonderful!"
The crowd applauded wildly as the
carnival master shook Jack Frost's

hand. "And what a wonderful costume!" he added.

Rachel, Kirsty, and Kylie watched as Jack Frost was pulled on stage by the carnival master. There was a storm of applause.

"Look, Jack Frost is blushing!" Kylie whispered.

It was true! Jack Frost was clearly enjoying all the attention. He had a smug look on his face.

"Please help me announce the winner," said the carnival master. Jack Frost looked even more pleased!

Rachel nudged Kirsty and pointed at the goblins, cheering in the front of the crowd.

The carnival master held up a piece of paper, and Jack Frost read: "Our carnival queen this year is Alexandra Kirby, for her beautiful princess costume!"

A little blond girl in a pretty princess outfit walked on stage, smiling. The carnival master helped her onto the golden throne, and then turned to Jack Frost for the crown.

Jack Frost frowned and clung to the crown when the carnival master tried to take it. But eventually, he had to let go. He couldn't do anything else in front of such a big audience.

As the carnival queen was crowned,
Jack Frost stomped sulkily off the stage.
Immediately, a crowd of children
surrounded him.

"Please can I have your autograph?"
asked one little boy.

"How did you find the crown?" asked
another.

"Can we take your picture?" begged
two little girls.

Looking flustered, Jack Frost tried
to move away, but the children
followed him.

"Jack Frost has a fan club!" Kylie said,
laughing, as she and the girls headed
away from the stage. "Girls, how can I
ever thank you? Now the Sunnydays
Carnival can move on,
and other children will
enjoy it."

"We were glad to help!" Rachel
smiled.

"And it must be almost time for the
fireworks," added Kirsty. "We'd
better go find Mom and Dad."

As she spoke, a huge, glittering cloud of fairy dust exploded in the air in front of them.

"Look, Kirsty!" Rachel gasped, as the dust began to clear. In front of them, the carousel was spinning and sparkling with fairy magic. And there, on a painted unicorn's back, sat King Oberon and Queen Titania.

Very Special Guests

"What are you doing here?" Rachel asked, thrilled as the Fairy King and Queen flew over to her.

"We've never seen you outside of Fairyland before," said Kirsty.

King Oberon smiled. "We came to thank you for all your help," he said.

"Thanks to you, the Sunnydays Carnival is saved!" added the queen.

"But what about Jack Frost?" Kirsty asked anxiously.

"Don't worry about him!" The king said, pointing at Jack Frost. He was happily signing autographs for all the children. "He's enjoying himself."

"Jack Frost loves to be the center of attention," the queen explained. "He's so popular right now that he won't cause any more trouble at the carnival."

"Come here!" Jack Frost was calling to his goblins. "Collect those autograph books and carnival programs. I'll sign them all!"

Rachel and Kirsty laughed.

"So the carnival's safe!" said Rachel.

"Yes, and we brought these to say thank you," Queen Titania replied. She lifted her wand and touched Kirsty's hand, then Rachel's. Suddenly, each girl found herself holding a tiny, glittering carousel!

"Look, Rachel," Kirsty gasped.
"They're exactly like the
Sunnydays carousel!"

"And the horses move
around, too!" Rachel
added, turning her
carousel. "They're
beautiful!"

A whooshing
noise made them
all look up, just
in time to see a
shower of red and
green sparks light
the sky.

"The fireworks
are starting," said
King Oberon. "You'd better
hurry back to Kirsty's parents, girls.

Kylie, the queen, and I have work
to do!"

Queen Titania smiled and winked at

Rachel and Kirsty. "We
have to make sure the
fireworks are extra-special
this year!" Kylie clapped
her hands in joy.
"Good-bye!" cried Rachel
and Kirsty. "And thank you
for our beautiful gifts."

The fairies waved their wands, and
then zoomed into the night sky in a
shower of colorful sparkles. Seconds later,
as the girls joined Kirsty's parents, the sky
filled with fireworks, glittering
in all the colors of the
rainbow.

· "Wow!" the carnival master gasped,
looking surprised. "I don't remember
buying such amazing fireworks!"

Rachel and Kirsty grinned at each
other. They were the only ones who
knew that a little fairy magic was adding
a lot of extra sparkle to the Sunnydays
Carnival!

RAINBOW magic™

The FUN DAY Fairies

The Fun Day Fairies are each responsible for adding spunk and sparkle to one day of the week! But when Jack Frost steals their magic, they need Rachel and Kirsty's help. Without the fairies' special flags, every day of the week will be gloomy and glum.

Coming in August 2008!

Take a sneak peek at . . .

Megan
the Monday
Fairy!

Off to Fairyland

"I'm glad I'm staying with you during vacation," Kirsty Tate told her best friend, Rachel Walker, as they came out of Fashion Fun, the accessories store on Tippington's Main Street. "And I hope these sparkly clips will look good with my new haircut!"

"I'm sure they will," Rachel said cheerfully. "They're so pretty."

"Thanks," Kirsty replied. "I wonder how the fairies are," she added, lowering her voice.

Rachel and Kirsty shared a magical secret: When they first met each other on a very special trip to Rainspell Island, they also became friends with the fairies!

"I hope Jack Frost and his goblins are behaving themselves," Rachel said.

Cold, wicked Jack Frost and his mean goblins often caused trouble for the fairies. But the girls had helped their tiny friends outwit Jack Frost many times.

"Look, Rachel!" Kirsty said, peering into a nearby window. "This store wasn't open the last time I was here. Isn't it great?"

The store was called Dancing Days, and the window was full of dance outfits and shoes. There were white tutus, satin ballet slippers with pink ribbons, and sparkly tap shoes.

"I'd love to be able to tap-dance," said Rachel.

Just then the door opened and a lady emerged, followed by a girl with a long brown ponytail.

The girl's face lit up when she saw Rachel. "Hi, Rachel!" she called.

"Hi, Karen," said Rachel with a smile. "Kirsty, this is Karen. She's my friend from school. And this is her mom, Mrs. Lewis."

Karen grinned at Kirsty. "It's nice to meet you," she said. "Rachel talks about you all the time!"

Kirsty laughed. "Are you learning to dance?" she asked, glancing at Karen's blue bag.

"Yes," Karen replied. "I have tap class at the town hall this afternoon, and Mom just bought me some new tap shoes. My old ones were worn out."

"That's because she practices so much!" Mrs. Lewis said, smiling. She glanced at her watch. "We'd better hurry, Karen."

"See you later!" Karen called as they left.

"Maybe you could sign up for Karen's tap classes," Kirsty suggested to Rachel as they walked down the street.

"Good idea," Rachel agreed. Then she glanced around. "Should we walk home through the park?"

"Sure!" Kirsty replied.

The girls walked through the iron park gate and across the grass. The park was filled with colorful flowers, and in the middle was a large brass sundial shining in the light.

"The sun's bright today," Kirsty said.

Rachel nodded. Then she noticed something that made her heart beat faster — tiny golden sparkles were hovering and dancing above the sundial!

"Kirsty, look at the sundial!" Rachel gasped. "I think it's fairy magic!"

Fairyland is never far away!
Look for these other

books:

The Rainbow Fairies

#1: Ruby the Red Fairy

#2: Amber the Orange Fairy

#3: Sunny the Yellow Fairy

#4: Fern the Green Fairy

#5: Sky the Blue Fairy

#6: Inky the Indigo Fairy

#7: Heather the Violet Fairy

The Weather Fairies

#1: Crystal the Snow Fairy

#2: Abigail the Breeze Fairy

#3: Pearl the Cloud Fairy

#4: Goldie the Sunshine Fairy

#5: Evie the Mist Fairy

#6: Storm the Lightning Fairy

#7: Hayley the Rain Fairy

The Jewel Fairies

#1: India the Moonstone Fairy

#2: Scarlett the Garnet Fairy

#3: Emily the Emerald Fairy

#4: Chloe the Topaz Fairy

#5: Amy the Amethyst Fairy

#6: Sophie the Sapphire Fairy

#7: Lucy the Diamond Fairy

The Pet Fairies

#1: Katie the Kitten Fairy

#2: Bella the Bunny Fairy

#3: Georgia the Guinea Pig Fairy

#4: Lauren the Puppy Fairy

#5: Harriet the Hamster Fairy

#6: Molly the Goldfish Fairy

#7: Penny the Pony Fairy

Special Editions

Joy the Summer Vacation Fairy

Holly the Christmas Fairy

Kylie the Carnival Fairy

Fairy Friends Sticker Book

Fairy Fashion Dress-Up Book

And look for the Fun Day Fairies in August 2008!

#1 Megan the Monday Fairy

#2 Tara the Tuesday Fairy

#3 Willow the Wednesday Fairy

#4 Thea the Thursday Fairy

#5 Felicity the Friday Fairy

#6 Sienna the Saturday Fairy

#7 Sarah the Sunday Fairy

A fairy for every day!

The seven Rainbow Fairies are missing! Help rescue the fairies and bring the sparkle back to Fairyland.

When mean Jack Frost steals the Weather Fairies' magical feathers, the weather turns wacky. It's up to the Weather Fairies to fix it!

Jack Frost is causing trouble in Fairyland again! This time he's stolen the seven crown jewels. Without them, the magic in Fairyland is fading fast!

■ SCHOLASTIC

FAIRY1

www.scholastic.com

Come flutter by Butterfly Meadow,
the new series by the creators of Rainbow Magic!

Butterfly Meadow #1: Dazzle's First Day

Dazzle is a new butterfly, fresh out of her cocoon. She doesn't know how to fly, and she's all alone! But Butterfly Meadow could be just what Dazzle is looking for.

Butterfly Meadow #2: Twinkle Dives In

Twinkle is feisty, fun, and always up for an adventure. But the nearby pond holds much more excitement than she expected!